THE ROOKIE TRAP

LEAGUE OF THE PARANORMAL

THE ROOKIE TRAP

CHRIS KREIE

DARBY CREEK
MINNEAPOLIS

Darby Creek
A division of Lerner Publishing Group, Inc.
241 First Avenue North
Minneapolis, MN 55401 USA

For reading levels and more information, look up this title at www.lernerbooks.com.

Image credits: stayorgo/Getty Images (house); bubaone/Getty Images (soccer ball); LoudRedCreative/Getty Images (texture); komkrit Preechachanwate/Shutterstock.com (texture).

Main body text set in Janson Text LT Std.
Typeface provided by Adobe Systems

Library of Congress Cataloging-in-Publication Data

Names: Kreie, Chris, author.
Title: The rookie trap / by Chris Kreie.
Description: Minneapolis : Darby Creek, [2019] | Series: League of the paranormal | Summary: "Before soccer practice, Molly's coach asks her to grab something from the equipment shed. But as soon as she enters, she gets trapped inside. Will Molly solve the mystery before anyone else gets trapped?"— Provided by publisher.
Identifiers: LCCN 2018059099 (print) | LCCN 2018061080 (ebook) | ISBN 9781541557000 (eb pdf) | ISBN 9781541556843 (lb : alk. paper) | ISBN 9781541572973 (pb : alk. paper)
Subjects: | CYAC: Soccer—Fiction. | Friendship—Fiction. | Blessing and cursing—Fiction. | Witchcraft—Fiction.
Classification: LCC PZ7.K8793 (ebook) | LCC PZ7.K8793 Roo 2019 (print) | DDC [Fic]—dc23

LC record available at https://lccn.loc.gov/2018059099

Manufactured in the United States of America
1-46118-43493-4/10/2019

1

Molly jumped high into the air with a burst
of energy. She timed her jump perfectly
and met the soccer ball with her forehead,
aiming it at the other team's goal, toward one
of her teammates in a red mesh jersey. She
immediately regained her footing and sprinted
for the middle of the field.

She was a midfielder. It was her natural
position. She was quick. She could attack,
but she could also defend. And she took more
pride in setting up teammates, in delivering
the perfect pass, than she did in scoring
goals. From an early age, she had learned that
midfielders were the players on a soccer team

who had to work the hardest, who had to run the most, and who had to have the most well-rounded skillset. She never backed away from a challenge. She wanted to be thought of as the toughest, fastest, most versatile player on the field. Midfield was the place for her.

It was the final day of tryouts for the Winchester Whitecaps. Molly had spent the last four days working her tail off, trying to impress the coach and the other players. She was new to town. Her mom had taken a job managing the local bank, which meant another move for the two of them. It was the fourth move for Molly since kindergarten. As a sophomore last year at her old high school, she had excelled on the junior varsity team. This year, her goal was to make varsity at Winchester High. Anything less would be a disappointment.

Molly raced toward the box. A teammate controlled the ball in the far right corner of the field. Molly kept one eye on the ball and another on her opponents in blue jerseys. If her teammate lost control of the ball, Molly would have to sprint back and join the defenders to make sure her opponents didn't make a strong counter and take the ball the other direction.

She also took a quick look at the goalie. Her name was Scarlett, and from what Molly had seen so far that week, she was a bit of an outcast. She stood out from the crowd with her partially shaven head, nose piercing, and thick black eye liner. She certainly didn't look like a typical jock. Molly hoped Scarlett's appearance wasn't the reason the other girls seemed to keep their distance from her. Molly suspected, instead, it was Scarlett's quiet nature and sullen disposition that caused the other girls to leave her alone.

Even if Scarlett wasn't much of a team player, she was a good goalie. She was tall and lanky, with long arms able to reach almost any ball that made it over her head.

Molly's teammate gained some space and kicked a strong ball into the box. Molly burst forward. She knocked the ball down with a high right foot, then made a great touch with her left. She spotted a teammate, Daneen, slipping past a defender to her left. Molly slid a perfect pass toward her, catching her in stride as she sprinted toward the goal. Daneen collected the ball, then immediately cocked her leg and sent a screamer toward the top-right corner of the goal. Scarlett didn't stand a chance. She fully extended her body, doing everything in her power to stop the shot, but only managed to get a fingertip on the ball. It flew over the goal line and hard into the webbing of the goal.

"Yes!" Molly screamed, then immediately raced over to Daneen.

"Sick pass, Molly!" Daneen yelled as Molly jumped into her arms.

"Way to finish," said Molly. The two of them exchanged a high five as other members of the red team came over to congratulate Daneen and Molly.

Just then Coach Rogers blew the whistle.

"Bring it in, girls!" she shouted from the sidelines.

Molly, Daneen, and the rest of the players jogged toward the sidelines. Molly stopped and waited for Scarlett to catch up. "Impossible goal to stop," said Molly.

Scarlett shook her head. "I should've had it," she grumbled quietly as the two of them walked toward their teammates.

"Next time." Molly smiled and draped an arm around Scarlett's shoulder.

Scarlett pulled back. "Save it," she said. "I don't need your pity."

Molly stopped walking. "I wasn't . . ." she said as Scarlett kept walking. Molly shook her head. *Jeez. I was just trying to be friendly.*

The girls gathered around Coach Rogers. "Time to announce the rosters for our teams," she shouted. "I'll do varsity first, and then JV. If you don't hear your name, I apologize in advance, but we don't have spots for everyone. I'll be in my office for a full hour after this, so if you want to talk about anything, that is your chance." Molly looked at the other players. There was obvious tension in the air.

Coach Rogers went on to list the sixteen players on the varsity team. Molly's heart was racing. Coach read one name after another for the varsity team. Daneen made it. So did Pooja, another girl Molly had gotten to know during the week. She was happy for both of them. But as Coach Rogers kept going, she began to worry. She had lost count the number of names, but she knew there could only be a few spots left. "Alex Edwards," said Coach Rogers. "Stephanie Stinson. Molly Porter." That was it! She'd made varsity. Molly could not contain her grin.

Coach Rogers continued. "And last on varsity, Maria Suarez."

"You've got to be kidding me!" someone shouted. Molly turned. It was Scarlett. Everyone looked at her. "How could I not make varsity?" Scarlett continued. "This is ridiculous. I'm the best goalie on this team."

"Watch yourself, Scarlett," said Coach Rogers. "There's still a place for you on JV. If you work hard and show me the right attitude, varsity could still be in your future."

Scarlett crossed her arms. "You never wanted me on this team."

"Not with the kind of behavior you're showing right now," said Coach. "Have you ever thought about that?"

"I'm out of here." Scarlett turned and marched away. "I don't need this."

"Scarlett, think about what you're doing!" shouted Coach Rogers. "Don't blow this opportunity! I expect to see you back on the field Monday!"

The rest of the girls let out a collective breath. Some of them broke out in nervous laughter.

"We'll pretend that didn't happen," said Coach Rogers. "But remember this. You can be a skilled player, but your performance comes down to your attitude. We're a team, both on and off the field."

Coach Rogers went on to read off the names from the JV team. When she was finished, there were smiles on the faces of many girls, but tears in the eyes of others. Molly felt the pain of the girls who didn't make the team.

"You should all feel proud. Cuts were extremely difficult this year." Coach paused for a moment before yelling, "Okay! That's all for now. Practice starts Monday."

The girls scattered to the sidelines to retrieve their bags. Immediately Pooja and Daneen rushed over to Molly. "Congratulations!" said Daneen.

"You too!" said Molly.

"It's going to be a good season," said Daneen.

"A great season," said Molly.

Pooja shrugged her shoulders. "Eh, it's going to be all right." She then flashed a huge smile.

Molly laughed and gave Pooja a playful shove. Then the three of them locked arms and walked off the field together. Molly's grin had yet to disappear.

2

Molly spent the entire weekend thinking about soccer. In bed Friday night. Doing chores Saturday morning. While eating dinner with her mom Sunday afternoon. She was excited, and nervous.

Practice finally rolled around Monday after school, and when it did, Molly's nerves took over. The players for the Whitecaps were good. Really good. And they were even stronger and faster than she remembered from tryouts. Molly quickly began to doubt her ability.

Playing for the Whitecaps was harder than she expected. Her teammates made very few mistakes, so any error Molly made stood out. She wondered if she had what it took to be a Whitecap. Add that to the fact that Coach Rogers was incredibly demanding. The team did nothing but run for the first half hour of practice. Molly thought she might throw up by the end of their tenth set of sprints. Coach Rogers demanded excellence. She was tough. And she was extremely loud.

"Faster!" barked Coach Rogers. "Quick feet! Control!" Molly was teamed up with Pooja for a passing drill. Four cones were set up in a square. Pooja sent passes to Molly as she moved back and forth between two cones. Molly's job was to collect the pass, make one touch to her other foot, dance around a cone, then push a pass back to Pooja. They repeated this routine over and over. "Come on Molly!" yelled her coach. "Quicker. Let's go!"

Molly took every pass from Pooja, trying to move her feet as quickly as she could. Her entire concentration was on the ball and the light footwork necessary to move the ball around the cones and get it back squarely on Pooja's foot. She could feel the beads of sweat trickling off her face. Suddenly her feet got tangled up and she went tumbling to the ground.

"Get up, Molly!" shouted Coach Rogers. "Come on. Two more!" Molly got quickly to her feet and received another pass. She danced around the cone. Then another. One last ball. She collected it, touched it over to her right foot, slipped easily around the cone, then sent a perfect pass back to Pooja.

"Not bad for a midfielder," said Pooja with a smile.

"I'll get it," said Molly as the two of them jogged toward the sidelines. "I just need more practice."

"You're doing fine," said Pooja. "Shake it off."

"Water!" shouted Coach Rogers. "Molly! Over here!"

Molly ran to her coach. "I need you to grab some practice goals from the equipment shed," said Coach Rogers. "Go get six of them, would you?"

"Sure." Molly looked around. "Where?"

"The shed's that way," said Coach Rogers. "Around the building." She pointed toward the school.

"Got it." Molly nodded and ran off.

She ran around the opposite side of the school. She wanted to be quick. She wanted to show Coach Rogers she could be counted on.

Once she made it to the other side of the school she scanned the grounds. She couldn't see anything except an open field and a group of boys from the football team going through drills. No equipment shed. Was she on the wrong side of the building?

Then she spotted something hidden in the bushes at the edge of the practice field. Sure enough, it was a shed. *But, it couldn't possibly be the shed Coach Rogers meant*, Molly thought. It was leaning awkwardly to one side, the roof covered in green moss. The white paint was chipping off. It looked like it could fall over at any minute. It had to be over a hundred years old.

Molly glanced around once more. This was the only shed she could see. It had to be the one.

She jogged over to it, then reached out and pulled at the latch. A group of crows who had been perched on top of the shed gave out loud caws and flew off. The sky suddenly darkened. Molly looked up to see a large, gray cloud move in front of the sun. *The sky was clear blue a minute ago*, she thought. *Where did that cloud come from?*

Molly was a bit freaked out. But she had a job to do. She didn't want to disappoint Coach Rogers. The door moaned and creaked as it opened. A musty stench of used equipment, mold, and rotten wood nearly knocked her over. She pulled her T-shirt up to cover her nose, then reluctantly stepped inside.

With no windows, it was difficult to see. The shed was not much bigger than her mom's backyard garden shed, but there was gear piled up in all directions. As she walked inside she nearly tripped over a wooden baseball bat. She shook her head. She had no idea how she was ever going to find the practice goals. *Coach should've given me a flashlight*, she thought.

As she turned to prop open the doors for more light, she heard a loud bang. The shed door had slammed shut. Suddenly she was in complete darkness. She couldn't see her hand in front of her face. Molly's heart began to pound. She hated the dark. And she hated tight spaces even more. One time she had gotten trapped in a hotel elevator during a power outage. It had lasted only a few minutes, but it had felt like forever.

"Don't panic," she told herself. "It's a creepy old equipment shed. Nothing more. Just open the door, grab the goals, and get out of here. You're fine."

She crept slowly toward the entrance, reaching her arms out in front of her. She eventually made it. She felt the rough wood of the door but couldn't find the latch. She couldn't feel any hinges or gaps. *What in the world?* she wondered. *Am I at the wrong wall? The door should definitely be here.*

Thinking maybe she'd moved diagonally across the shed instead of straight back, Molly moved from the corner to another wall. The door had to be there. She took short, measured steps. She didn't want to trip over anything again. But then she realized there was no longer anything on the floor. It was like all the junk inside the shed had disappeared. Her heart began thumping even harder. *Something's wrong.*

Molly felt for the door on the next wall. Nothing. No door. Then she moved on to the next. After a few seconds she had made a complete loop around the entire equipment shed. There was no door latch.

There was no door.

She continued to frantically scurry around the shed, her heart in her throat. "Molly, you're making things worse," she said. "Calm down."

It was then she felt as if the walls were closing in on her. The shed suddenly seemed much smaller than it was before. She could actually stand in the middle of it and easily touch all four walls. *This is impossible*, she thought. *I must be losing my mind.*

Then the truly terrifying happened. The floor beneath Molly's feet began to fall away. She was being swallowed up by the ground.

That can't be! She felt for the walls. Her fingers slipped. She was definitely dropping.

"Help!" she shrieked. "Help me! Please! I'm in the shed! Somebody help me!"

She continued to drop into the ground, her hands clutching against the walls. She frantically reached for something to grab onto. Something she could use to pull herself out of the hole.

This must be a dream, Molly thought. *How is this possible?*

She felt dirt closing around her hips. Then her waist. Her shoulders. She tried moving her body. She was completely stuck. Molly finally felt the dirt creeping up her neck. "Help! Please!" she screamed. She thought she might be breathing her last breath.

But then, just when Molly felt the dirt piling up over her chin, a bright burst of light filled the shed. The sensation of dropping into the ground, the sensation of being surrounded by dirt, instantly disappeared.

Molly looked toward the light. She had to shield her eyes. Two tall bodies stood at the door. It was Pooja and Daneen. Molly quickly looked around. She was crouched low to the ground. In a ball. Piles of old equipment surrounded her. There was no dirt to be seen.

Daneen reached inside. "Molly!" she cried. "Get out of there. Now!" Molly got to her feet, and Daneen forcefully pulled her from the shed.

3

"Are you okay?" asked Daneen. Molly had immediately collapsed onto the ground after Daneen pulled her from the shed.

Molly lay in the grass, staring at the bright sky. The dark clouds that had been there mere moments ago were gone.

"Molly," said Daneen. "Can you hear me?"

She closed her eyes and took in a deep breath. "I can hear you," she said. "I'm fine." She took a couple more breaths, feeling her heart rate slow, then finally pushed herself up to a seated position.

"We panicked when Coach Rogers told us she had sent you to grab equipment and when you hadn't come back after almost fifteen minutes," said Daneen.

"*Fifteen?*" said Molly. "I left practice barely two minutes ago." None of this was making any sense. "Wait. Why, exactly, did you guys freak out? Did you know I was in trouble?"

Pooja and Daneen looked at each other. "It's complicated," said Daneen.

"Girls!" Coach Rogers had appeared from around the corner of the building. "Get back to practice!"

Looking across the field at Coach Rogers, Molly spotted a large, white equipment shed next to the school. It was plain as day. *How in the world had I missed that?* she thought. *I swear that wasn't there before.*

"We should've told you," said Daneen. "The first day you made the team. We're so sorry."

"You should've told me what?" asked Molly.

"You're not going to believe us," said Pooja.

"Hey, after what just happened to me back there, I think I'll believe anything," said Molly.

"It's cursed," said Daneen. "There. I said it. The shed is cursed."

"Cursed?" asked Molly.

"Girls!" shouted Coach Rogers. "Now!"

"Come to my house after practice," said Daneen as the three of them finally began jogging toward the Coach Rogers. "We'll explain everything."

4

Later that night, the three girls sat together in Daneen's bedroom. "Should we get right to it?" asked Daneen.

"No," said Molly. "I almost died today, but I have an idea. Let's chat about our favorite brand of nail polish or who we have a crush on instead."

Pooja laughed.

"Sorry," said Daneen.

"OK," said Pooja. "Get comfortable. This isn't a quick story."

Molly settled into a beanbag chair in the corner of the room. "I'm ready."

Pooja began. "All right. The story goes that around sixty years ago, a group of girls from

Winchester started a soccer team. Remember, soccer for girls at the time did not exist. So this team became famous around town. They were like pioneers, and they traveled around the state competing against boys teams and supposedly doing pretty well. They actually won more games than they lost.

"But then, there was this one girl. Her name was Vivian Cooper. She really wanted to play on the team but the other girls wouldn't let her."

"Why not?" asked Molly.

"Apparently she was an exceptional athlete," Pooja continued. "But nobody liked her. She was shunned by the other girls. Her family was dirt-poor and lived in a tiny, run-down shack in the hills above town. She'd usually show up at school smelling bad in ratty clothes and with snarls in her hair. There was even a local legend that the women in Vivian's family were witches. Every other girl at Winchester High kept their distance from her.

"Finally, one day," Pooja continued. "The girls from the soccer team told Vivian she could play with them. But the joke was on her. The girls had no intention of letting her on the team. Instead, after asking Vivian to go into the shed for some equipment, they locked her inside and left her there. She was in there for days."

"That's awful," said Molly. Daneen nodded.

Pooja went on. "Back then, people thought she'd been abducted. Or murdered. The town was shaken. As far as everyone knew, a girl from Winchester had just up and disappeared. People went crazy. Everyone worried their child would be next."

"Didn't the girls from the team ever tell anyone?" asked Molly.

"Well, a few days later, the police received an anonymous note that Vivian was in the shed," said Pooja. "But here's the thing." She leaned forward. "When they broke open the lock and went inside, it was empty."

"Vivian had disappeared," said Daneen.

"But," Pooja said, "scratched into one of the walls were the words, 'I will never forget.'"

"To this day, Vivian's body hasn't been found," said Daneen.

"So none of those girls ever confessed to locking her in the shed?" asked Molly.

"Nope," said Pooja. "Not one."

"Then how do you know for sure that's what happened?" asked Molly.

"We don't," said Daneen. "But that's the story everyone tells. It's the story that's been told for decades."

"Wow." Molly sat back and let it sink in. "So what about the curse?"

"Vivian put a curse on the shed," said Pooja. She looked at Daneen, then back at Molly. "Are you ready for this?"

"Tell me," said Molly.

"This is the freaky part," said Pooja.

"Tell me already!"

"We're the only ones who can see the shed."

"What to do you mean?" asked Molly. "And who's 'we?'"

"The players," said Pooja. "The girls from the soccer team. We're the only ones who can see it."

"After Vivian disappeared, the town tore down the shed and built the new one," said

Daneen. "For everyone else, the old shed doesn't exist. It's invisible."

"Come on," said Molly. "But I saw it. I touched it. I got trapped inside of it."

"Did you?" asked Daneen. "Are you sure about that?"

Molly's head was spinning. *Could everything Pooja and Daneen are saying be true?* "It sure felt real," she said.

"I'm sure it did," said Pooja. "Believe me, you're not the first one to experience it. After Vivian disappeared, over the next few decades, several other girls from the Winchester soccer team went missing. We think they vanished after going into the shed."

"We think Vivian's curse makes the new equipment shed disappear temporarily," said Daneen. "The one Coach sent you to get the goals from."

"Then Vivian lures new players into the other shed and locks them inside forever," said Pooja. "It's like a trap for rookies."

"Okay," said Molly. "So nail the door shut. Or tear it down again. Make sure no other girls go in there. My mom has a sledgehammer in the garage. Let's go do it right now."

Pooja and Daneen laughed. "You think no one else has ever thought of that?" asked Daneen.

"The shed doesn't exist, remember?" said Pooja. "Other girls have tried that. They've locked the door. They've destroyed it. The next day the shed just comes back, the same as it was before."

"Some girls over the years have even made the mistake of telling their parents or their coach," said Daneen. "Imagine trying to convince an adult we're being cursed by an old witch with an invisible shed . . ."

"So what then?" asked Molly. "What do we do?"

"We stay away from the shed," said Daneen. "It's as simple as that. And we tell no one outside the team. The players have been doing that for the past twenty years, and so far, it's worked. Not one other girl has gone missing since then. The secret remains with us."

"We just didn't tell you soon enough," said Daneen. "We were planning to after practice."

"And everyone else on the team knows?" asked Molly.

"That's the job of upperclassmen," said Pooja. "To tell new members of the team. To make sure they take the curse seriously and stay far away from the shed."

"You forgot to tell her one thing," said Daneen.

"Oh right," said Pooja. "We're pretty sure Vivian's curse affects the team on the field too."

"Oh, is that all," said Molly.

"Winchester hasn't had a winning season since Vivian disappeared," Pooja.

"Great," said Molly.

"But we're going to end that part of the curse this year," said Daneen. "This year we're going to the playoffs." She sat down next to Molly and wrapped an arm around her. "Isn't that right?"

"That's right!" said Pooja from across the bedroom. "Molly, you're our new secret weapon. Vivian's curse is no match for us. This year we're going places!"

All Molly could do was shake her head and muster a weak smile. "Out of all the schools in America, my mom chooses the one with an equipment shed cursed by a vengeful, angry witch with a long memory and an inability to forgive."

The other two laughed. "That's right," said Pooja. She came over and joined the others in the beanbag.

Daneen grinned. "We're glad she did."

5

The rest of the week Molly tried her best to put the shed and the curse of Vivian Cooper out of her mind. It wasn't easy. The only thing that worked was to put all her focus and energy toward soccer. *Stay away from the shed and tell no one*, she continued to tell herself. *Play soccer and forget about the ridiculous curse.*

A week after their conversation at Daneen's house, the Whitecaps had their first game of the season. They played the Raiders from nearby Derry.

Molly did some last-minute stretching as she and her teammates waited for the referee to blow the whistle and the Raiders to take the kickoff. "Let's do this thing," Molly said. She'd been anxiously awaiting this moment since she moved to Winchester.

Tweet!

A player from Derry kicked the ball backwards to a teammate who immediately sent it forward, up the right sideline to a teammate streaking toward the Whitecaps' goal. Molly raced over to defend. She was met by a Whitecaps defender. Together they wrestled control of the ball away from the Raider. Molly took off in the other direction and her teammate on defense passed her the ball.

Molly looked up. She had some room in front of her to dribble and move the ball to midfield. She spotted Pooja racing forward on the opposite side of the field. Molly collected the ball, then sent a long pass toward Pooja.

Pooja expertly knocked the ball down with her chest, then dribbled it into the corner. A Raider defender was all over her, but Pooja managed to dribble past her. The defender had no choice but to desperately reach her foot out and tackle the ball over the goal line.

"Yes," said Molly. "Corner kick." The Whitecaps would have an early opportunity to score.

The team had spent time recently practicing corner kicks. In games, Pooja would take the corners from the right side, Daneen from the left. Molly's job was to get into the box and make a play on the ball. If the other team managed to control the ball, it was Molly's responsibility to scurry back on defense to help prevent a counter attack.

Pooja placed the ball in the corner arc, then raised her arm above her head. Molly and her teammates fought for position in and around the box. The referee blew her whistle.

Pooja sent the corner kick high into the box. Molly watched its flight. She was in great position. The ball was curling straight toward her. She would barely have to move to make a play on the ball.

A Raider slid over, defending her perfectly, putting a body on Molly. As the ball sailed toward her, Molly wondered if she'd have a chance at a shot. Her defender was all over her.

She and the Raider defender jumped at exactly the same moment. *Get your head on the ball*, she quickly thought. *You can jump higher than she can.*

Molly timed her leap well. She got a great push off the ground. She could feel herself rising into the air higher than anyone else around her. The ball was on her. She pushed her head into it and sent the ball toward the far left corner.

The ball slammed off the right post. She had missed a goal by inches.

She fell to the ground and watched the rest from there. It was a bit like slow motion. She could see the action through the legs and arms of the other players around her. The ball had ricocheted back in front of the goal and Daneen pounced on it. She gave it a slight touch to her left to avoid a defender, then kicked the ball hard. The goalie was on her back. The goal was completely open.

But Daneen missed it, too. She missed the easy shot. She kicked it too hard and too high, and her shot banged hard off the crossbar. It bounced back onto the field and was cleared out of bounds easily by a Raiders player.

Molly got to her feet and jogged over to Daneen.

"We'll get a goal," said Molly. "Next time. Keep your head up."

"It's that stupid curse," said Daneen. "I'm telling you. There's no way I should've missed that shot."

"Shake it off," Molly said then jogged back into position. *Could Daneen be right?* she wondered. *Was Vivian's curse really that strong? Did it really just cause both of us to miss our shots?* She hoped not. Otherwise, it was going to be a very long season.

6

The Whitecaps fell apart after that. Molly missed another scoring opportunity midway through the first half, and in the second half, Pooja twisted her ankle and had to be pulled from the game. Several balls bounced perfectly the Raiders' way, and their players capitalized on every easy opportunity. The game finished 3–0 with the win going to the Raiders.

After a post-game talk by Coach Rogers, Molly and her teammates dejectedly collected their gear and began the slow walk toward the school. It was then Molly spotted the JV team, still playing their game on a nearby field.

"I'll see you guys inside," said Molly as she left the group and jogged over to the other field. She watched the final minutes of the JV game, which they lost 2–1. Scarlett looked good, making a couple of nice stops to keep things close. When it was over, Molly waited for her.

"Tough loss," Molly said with a smile.

"We should've won," said Scarlett curtly.

"You looked good," said Molly. "If you keep playing like that, Coach will definitely move you up to varsity."

"We'll see."

They walked toward the school together.

Molly changed the subject. "Winchester is pretty cool," she said. "I'm starting to like it here. I've moved around a lot, and this is a place where I wouldn't mind staying."

"Winchester is pathetic," said Scarlett.

"Harsh," said Molly.

Scarlett looked surprised. "Sorry. It's just . . . you haven't been here long enough. I've lived here my whole life and I'm tired of everybody knowing everybody else and people always getting into each other's business. I can't wait to get out of this place."

"I'm not trying to get into your business," said Molly. "I'm just trying to be friendly."

"I know," said Scarlett. "I'm sorry. I put up walls." She chuckled and rolled her eyes. "At least that's what my therapist tells me."

Molly smiled back. "Don't worry about it." She kicked at the ground as they walked, unearthing a small rock that she sent sailing ahead a few yards. "Therapy, huh?"

"For my temper," said Scarlett. "You saw it."

"I used to go to therapy, too," said Molly. "Back when my parents got divorced. I was a mess."

"My guy's Dr. Waters," said Scarlett. "But he makes me call him Steve."

Molly laughed. "Mine was Claire. She was good. She helped me a lot."

"Steve's all right." Scarlett laughed.

Molly kicked at the rock again. "Hey," she said. "I sometimes do homework at that coffee house in town. We should study there together sometime."

"I hate coffee," said Scarlett.

"Okay," said Molly.

"But I kind of like tea."

"Then tea it is."

"Cool," said Scarlett.

"Great," said Molly. "I could definitely use help with French."

"I'm pretty good at that," said Scarlett.

"All right," said Molly. "A study session it is. See you around, then?"

Scarlett nodded. "For sure."

Molly turned and jogged toward school.

7

Later that week Molly was back at Daneen's house. They were sitting side by side on Daneen's bed. Pooja was on the beanbag, stuffing bright orange cheese balls into her mouth.

"Take it easy with those things," said Daneen. "You're such a junk food junkie."

"Coach would not be happy," said Molly. She held up her phone to take a picture of Pooja.

"Stop it!" Pooja turned her body away from Molly. "Okay, okay. I'm done. Jeez."

"Hey," said Molly. "I talked with that girl Scarlett the other day after our game."

Daneen gave Molly a sideways look. "You did what?"

"I saw her after the JV game," said Molly. "I felt bad about her not making varsity. I thought it would be nice to say hello."

"You talked to Scary Scarlett?" asked Pooja. "How did that go?"

"We're going to study together sometime. What do you guys have against . . ." Molly stopped. "Hold on. You call her Scary Scarlett?"

"Yeah," said Daneen. "You've seen her. She's freaky. She's all dark and brooding. And she never talks to anyone."

"Maybe that's because no one ever talks to her," said Molly.

"You really want to hang out with that girl?" asked Daneen. She and Pooja shared a disapproving glance.

"Nobody likes her," said Pooja. "She's an outcast. Do you like those kind of people?"

"Those kind of people?" asked Molly.

"It's just," said Daneen. "If you start hanging out with people like Scarlett, girls on the team might not want to hang out with you."

"When you say girls from the team, do you mean the two of you?" asked Molly. She suddenly felt very defensive.

"No, that's not what I'm saying," said Daneen. "Just be careful, that's all."

"She's called Scary Scarlett for a reason," said Pooja. "You saw how she reacted when she didn't get a place on the varsity team. You can't tell me that wasn't scary."

"Besides," said Daneen. "There's still one thing we haven't told you."

"Oh yeah?" said Molly. "And what's that?"

"She's a Cooper," said Pooja.

Molly sat up on the bed. "Wait a minute. Scarlett's last name is Cooper? Like Vivian Cooper?"

"The same," said Daneen. "Vivian's like, her great aunt or something."

"The Cooper women are witches," said Pooja. "Vivian was. Scarlett's probably one, too."

"You don't really believe that, do you?" asked Molly.

"Can you explain getting stuck in the shed last week?" asked Pooja.

She had a point. Molly thought for a second. She knew what had happened to her in the shed was real. *But Scarlett a witch? It couldn't be.*

"Makes you wish you never talked to her, doesn't it?" asked Daneen.

Molly sat in silence. The wheels in her head began to spin. *Scarlett is Vivian's niece,* she thought. *That could be really important. I wonder if we . . .*

"Hello." Daneen snapped her fingers in front of Molly's face. "Earth to Molly."

"Sorry," said Molly. "I was just thinking."

"Clearly," said Pooja.

Molly didn't care how Daneen and Pooja felt about Scarlett. She didn't care what they'd think if she was nice to her. Her mind was on the curse. And finding a way to break it.

8

Molly walked into study hall the next day and spotted Scarlett in the back row.

Molly approached her. "Mind if I sit?"

"No problem," said Scarlett.

Molly took the seat next to her. She looked at Scarlett's textbook. "Chemistry, huh? That class isn't too bad."

"I guess," Scarlett said. "The lighting things on fire part is okay."

Molly laughed. She unzipped her backpack and pulled out her US History textbook. She opened it up and pretended to read. What she wanted to do was ask Scarlett about her great aunt and the curse.

She flipped through a few pages, glancing over at Scarlett from time to time. After a few minutes of stalling and scanning the pages of her textbook, she grew impatient. "So, Vivian Cooper was your aunt?"

Scarlett rolled her eyes. "I wondered when you'd find out," she said. "This town is the worst."

"So it's true?"

Scarlett glared at Molly. "Yes, it's true. I'm the niece of Vivian Cooper, the Witch of Winchester?" She slammed her book shut. "You're just like everyone else. And here I thought maybe you'd be different." Scarlett grabbed her book and began to get up.

"Wait." Molly grabbed her arm. "I'm not like everyone else. Really. I was serious when I said I want to be your friend. When I said we should hang out."

"Then why all the questions about my aunt?" asked Scarlett. "I'm not her. I never even knew her."

"I'm sorry," said Molly. "I know you're not like her."

"Then what?" asked Scarlett. "Why do you want to talk about her?"

"I feel bad for what happened to Vivian," said Molly. "What those girls did to her was terrible. I'd like to do something about it."

"The new girl comes to town and saves the day," said Scarlett sarcastically. "You really think you can erase decades of torment and shame with a wave of your pretty hand?" She scoffed. "Or I get it. You feel sorry for me. That's it, isn't it?"

"No, that's not it at all," said Molly. "Will you at least just hear me out? I really want to help."

Scarlett waited.

"Please," pleaded Molly.

Scarlett relented and finally sat back down. "This better be good."

Molly continued her pitch. "You hate being associated with the curse of Vivian Cooper, right?"

"You noticed?" Scarlett scoffed.

"Well, I haven't told you this," said Molly. "But I got trapped inside that old equipment shed. The one Vivian supposedly put a curse

44

on. I felt like I was getting sucked into the ground. I thought I was going to die."

"Are you serious?" asked Scarlett.

"I am," said Molly. "It was terrifying."

"You know I don't have anything to do with the curse, right?" said Scarlett. "I can't control it."

"I know."

Scarlett shook her head. "I'm sorry that happened to you."

"Sorry enough to want to do something about it?" asked Molly.

Scarlett gave Molly a puzzled look.

"We break the curse," said Molly. "You and me. I want to make sure what happened to me in that shed never happens to another player. And you want to put an end to your family curse, right? Together maybe we can end this thing once and for all."

"You think I care about some bratty, entitled soccer players?" asked Scarlett. "You saw how they treated me."

"You can't honestly tell me you'd be happy if more girls went missing," said Molly.

Scarlett folded her arms across her chest. "Okay, maybe I don't want any of them to disappear. But I'm not sure I want to help them either."

"Think of it this way. You're not helping them. You're doing this for yourself. And your family. This is your chance to put the curse behind you. Forever."

Scarlett was silent for a moment, then let out a deep sigh. "Okay, fine. But it's not to help the soccer team. I'm doing this for the Coopers."

"Good," said Molly. "Then it's settled. You and I are going to end the curse of Vivian Cooper once and for all."

9

The Whitecaps played their second game of the season a couple days later. This time they were on the road playing the Princeton Tigers. In the second half, the game was deadlocked at 0–0.

"You all right?" Daneen shouted from across the field.

"I'm fine!" yelled Molly. She was on the ground. It was the third time in the game that she'd tripped and fallen. This time, as she picked herself up, she actually had to remove grass and clumps of dirt from her face. Seconds earlier she had been defending a Tigers player when her legs somehow got tangled up beneath her. Luckily the Tiger had dribbled the ball out of bounds.

As one of Molly's teammates prepared for the throw-in, she thought about what had happened. She'd been running in stride. She'd been perfectly keeping up with the player she was defending. She remembered preparing to tackle the ball away. She was in great position. Then suddenly, for absolutely no reason, she had tripped. Her feet just went out from under her.

It has to be the curse, she thought. *There's no other explanation.*

The throw-in came to Molly. She collected it and scanned the field. "Switch it!" called Pooja from the right side. Molly dribbled along the left side of the field. She and Pooja were both near the halfway line, moving slowly toward the Tigers' goal. Molly planted her foot and then sent the ball high and wide across the field to her. Pooja gave it a touch to collect it, then began a slow dribble forward along the right sideline. Molly jogged toward the center of the field to give her support.

As Molly jogged that way, she reached up and wiped sweat from her face. The temperature that afternoon was brutal. It was over 90 degrees, there was no wind, and the sun was beating down hard on the field. Molly took a deep breath and continued running forward.

Pooja's defender made a play on the ball, knocking it away from her and over the sidelines. "I've got it!" called Molly running over. This time she would take the throw-in.

She picked up the ball, then positioned herself on the sidelines, holding the ball with both hands above her head and surveying the field. Pooja, Daneen, and the rest of Molly's teammates fought to get clear of their defenders. Daneen made a break toward the middle of the field. Molly fired the ball in her direction. Almost immediately, a Tiger defender stepped in front of the pass and stole the ball away.

"Sorry!" called Molly rushing back to defend. "My bad!"

Molly sprinted in the other direction to defend against a Tiger player racing quickly down the sidelines towards the corner of the field. The Tiger with the ball sent a pass over Molly's head and deep into the corner. It was a footrace for the ball. Molly put her head down and ran with all her might to get to the corner before the Tiger player did.

She and the Tiger got to the spot at exactly the same time. The Tiger immediately turned her back to Molly and used her body to shield Molly from the ball. Molly didn't have a clear shot to poke the ball away unless she went through the Tiger player. That could result in a penalty and a potentially disastrous free kick.

The rest of the players from both teams were setting themselves up near the goal. Molly pushed against the Tiger player. She could be a physical player too. She'd wait until the right moment, then strike.

The Tiger continued to back in. Molly continued to push back. Finally, the player leaned into Molly a little too hard. Molly used the player's momentum to her advantage. She took a quick step backward. The Tiger player, having expected resistance from Molly, fell to the ground.

The ball was free. Molly pounced on it. She kicked it clear of the other player, then dribbled it up the sidelines in the other direction. She approached the halfway line and spotted Pooja, clear in the middle of the field. She drove a hard pass toward her.

Pooja got the ball perfectly in stride. She was in the open, moving directly toward the Tigers' goal.

Molly moved toward the center a bit, keeping some distance between herself and Pooja in order to avoid drawing her defender toward the ball. She could see Daneen doing the same thing on the left side of the field.

Two more Tiger defenders raced over to cover Pooja. She had no choice but to give up the ball.

"I'm open!" called Molly. Pooja sent the ball to her.

Molly raised her right foot to trap it. Then she immediately pushed the ball wide to avoid the defender. She looked across the field.

Daneen was moving into the box. A well-timed pass could set her up for a perfect shot.

Molly cocked back her leg, then blasted it forward. Her foot sped toward the ball.

But then, just as she expected her foot to make contact with the ball, her other foot slipped from under her.

Molly's weight went backwards. Her kicking leg went high, missing the ball completely. A split second later she was on her back, looking up at the sky.

A Tiger snatched the ball and the play moved to the other side of the field.

The grass wasn't wet. The turf was in perfect condition. *The curse*, thought Molly. *The stupid curse.* She sprang to her feet and ran back into the action.

10

The game remained tight the rest of the way with the Whitecaps doing everything they could to score. But they had no such luck. After another sweaty, exhausting half battling for the ball, the referee finally checked her watch, raised her arm into the air, and blew her whistle. The game was over.

Molly collapsed onto the ground. The game had ended in a 0–0 tie. Vivian's curse had once again kept the Whitecaps from winning.

A few minutes later the girls grabbed some water and collected their bags. "You're a true Whitecap now," Daneen said to Molly. "The curse really got to you out there."

"Aren't you guys tired of this?" asked Molly. "Aren't you tired of losing, and tired of the curse?"

"Sure," said Daneen.

"But what are we supposed to do about it?" asked Pooja.

"End it," said Molly. "End the curse. Put it behind this team and this town for good."

"And you think you know how to do that?" asked Daneen.

"I'm sure going to try," said Molly. "I'm meeting Scarlett tonight. At the shed." She looked across the field and saw Scarlett and the rest of the JV team walking toward the team bus.

"You're what?" asked Pooja. "I think I must be suffering from heatstroke." She held the back of her hand to her forehead. "It sounded like you just said you're meeting Scary Scarlett at the shed tonight."

"That is what I said," said Molly. "But stop calling her that."

"Why in the world are you going to the shed?" asked Daneen.

"Scarlett and I are planning to look for clues," said Molly. "To see if we can figure out a way to lift the curse. I was actually hoping both of you would join us."

Pooja scoffed. "Are you kidding?"

"You can't beat the curse," said Daneen. "Didn't you hear me the other night? Other players have tried. Nothing works. Besides, Vivian's not going to like it. Something really bad could happen to you guys."

"We're not going to mess with the shed," said Molly. "Or try to destroy it. We're just going to investigate. Don't you guys want to break the curse of Vivian Cooper?"

"Uh, not really," said Pooja. "I just want to stay away from the creepy shed and pretend it doesn't exist."

"Even after what happened to me?" asked Molly. "I could've disappeared forever, just like those other girls. Think about it. What if another player wanders in there like I did?"

Pooja and Daneen looked at each other. "It won't happen," said Daneen. "We just have to make sure all the players know about the curse."

"All it takes is one mistake," said
Molly. "I don't know about you guys, but I
couldn't live with myself knowing I could've
done something to stop a teammate from
disappearing in that shed."

"I'd love to end the curse," said Daneen.
"But what makes you think we can do it when
no one else before us could?"

"We're smarter than everyone else,"
said Molly.

Daneen rolled her eyes.

"You said it yourself," said Molly. "People
have tried to lock the shed or tear it down.
That's not what we want to do. We don't want
to destroy the shed. We want to piece the clues
together to end the curse and let Vivian rest
peacefully once and for all. Has anyone ever
tried doing that?"

Daneen shuffled her feet. "Not that I
know of."

"What clues?" asked Pooja.

"The message," said Molly. "The one
Vivian carved into the wall. 'I will never
forget.' She wrote that message for a reason.

Maybe she left other clues behind, too. Clues no one else has put together yet."

"I don't know, Molly," said Daneen. "I'm scared. What if you're wrong?"

"Think about it," said Molly. "You guys and the rest of the team are treating Scarlett the same way those girls treated Vivian seventy years ago. Maybe part of ending the curse is finally being nice to a Cooper."

Daneen and Pooja looked at each other.

"All I know is that we need to break this curse," says Molly. "One way or another. And I'm going to the shed tonight to try. With or without you guys."

11

Two hours later Molly walked alone across the school practice field. The sun had set behind the dark green hills west of town a few minutes earlier, and the heat of the day had lifted. The ground beneath her feet was already covered in dew. She could feel the wetness seeping through her shoes. Molly tucked her hands into her shorts pockets and wished she had worn a jacket.

She looked to the sky. The moon was full. It shone brightly above the tree line. *Of course there's a full moon*, she thought. *What's next? Howling wolves? Bats?*

As she approached the shed, she could see

that Scarlett was already there. "Hey."

"Hey," said Scarlett.

Molly opened up her arms and walked forward to embrace her. Scarlett put up her hands to stop her. "Um, no thanks," said Scarlett.

"Too much?" asked Molly.

"Too much," said Scarlett.

Molly quickly tried to move past the awkward moment. "Are you ready for this?" Molly asked, taking a step backwards.

"Why not," said Scarlett. Then she looked over Molly's shoulder. "What are they doing here?"

Molly turned. Walking toward them were Daneen and Pooja. Molly smiled and ran to them, sweeping them up in a big hug. "I wasn't sure you'd come," she said.

"Thank her," said Pooja looking at Daneen. "I don't know how she talked me into this."

The three of them approached the shed. "Hi Scarlett," said Daneen.

Scarlett didn't respond. Instead she scowled and looked at Molly. "You invited these two?"

"I did," said Molly. "I know the history between you guys isn't great."

"But we want to help," said Daneen.

"Really," said Scarlett sarcastically.

"They do," said Molly. "That's why they're here. We all want to break this curse."

"We're in this together," said Daneen. "And we're sorry for how we've treated you in the past." She looked at Pooja. "Isn't that right?" Daneen elbowed her.

"Um, yeah," said Pooja. "That's right."

Scarlett looked away. The four of them stood in silence. Molly thought about putting her hand on Scarlett's shoulder as a way to comfort her. But she quickly remembered her awkward hug attempt a moment ago and stopped. Instead she simply said, "You can trust us."

"I trust you," said Scarlett. "Barely." She nodded at Pooja and Daneen. "I don't trust them."

Molly nodded. "I get it," she said. "But they're here. And we're here. Can we put the past behind us for now and see what we can do to end this curse?"

Scarlett kicked at the dirt.

"Hey," said Pooja. "We're trying to be nice to you. Don't you get that?"

"You've never been nice to me," Scarlett snapped back.

"Whoa. Relax."

"Don't tell me to relax!"

"There's that anger again."

Scarlett looked at Molly. "See what I'm talking about?" she said. "It's always the same with them."

Molly pulled her aside. "Don't listen to Pooja. She's harmless. But she's also nice when you get to know her. Pooja and Daneen could be your friends if you gave them a chance and opened up a little more."

"I don't want to be their friends," said Scarlett.

"Okay," sighed Molly. "Then let's not worry about that right now. We're here for the curse. Let's just keep our focus on that. You do want to end your family curse, don't you?"

"Of course."

"Just forget about Pooja and Daneen for now," said Molly. "And do what we came here to do."

Scarlett looked up and sighed. "All right."

"Good," said Molly, smiling. "Then let's get to it."

12

The four girls approached the shed.

"You two chickens can stay out here and hold the door open," said Scarlett, reaching to open the latch. "Molly and I will go inside."

"Sounds good to me," said Pooja.

Molly pulled a flashlight out of her backpack and flicked it on. Scarlett did the same. As Pooja and Daneen held the door wide open, Molly and Scarlett slowly entered the shed.

Except for the beams of their flashlights, the inside of the shed was pure darkness. Molly felt a shiver go through her body. The memory of the incident from two weeks earlier, the walls closing in on her, was a little too fresh. It all came flooding back. The sensation of being trapped. The feeling of the ground falling away below her feet. The dirt closing around her neck. She never wanted to feel those things ever again. She wondered if it was a huge mistake to come back.

Molly pushed those thoughts out of her mind. She reminded herself that what they were doing was important.

"You guys find anything yet?" shouted Daneen from outside. "We can't see a thing from out here."

"Not yet!" Molly shouted back, then stepped deeper into the shed. She picked her way through piles of old baseball bats, wooden tennis rackets, and deflated footballs. Scarlett was behind her, shining the beam of her flashlight in all directions.

Molly lifted a stack of softball bases off the ground. She looked through a pile of football pads. She wasn't sure what she was looking for.

"Check this out," said Scarlett.

Molly turned. Scarlett held the beam of her flashlight on some words scratched into the wall.

"It's Vivian's message," said Scarlett. "The one she carved when she was stuck inside here."

Molly shuddered. In front of her were the words, *I will never forget.* It was the message Vivian had left behind. *Exactly like the story,* she thought.

"I can't even imagine how Aunt Vivian must have felt," said Scarlett. "Being trapped inside here."

"It must have been awful." Molly turned away from the wall. She didn't want her mind to drift back to her own experience in the shed. She pressed forward.

After they poked around for a few more minutes, Scarlett said, "Come help me with this."

Molly turned. "What is it?" Shining her light in that direction, Molly could see Scarlett with her hands on a large sheet of plywood. It was leaning against the wall, and it was so big that it looked like the actual wall itself.

Molly stepped over to help Scarlett.

"Let's lift it away," said Scarlett. Molly grabbed hold. "One, two, three."

"Ugh!" Molly grunted. The board was stuck. There were piles of old equipment wedged up against it. It wouldn't move.

"One more time," said Scarlett. "Here we go. One, two, pull!"

They pulled with everything they had. Again, nothing.

"We're going to need your help!" Scarlett called.

Pooja and Daneen poked their heads inside.

Scarlett tossed an old football helmet out through the door. "Prop open the door with that," she said.

"I'm not going in there," said Pooja. "No way."

"Settle down," said Daneen, putting the helmet in front of the door. "Nothing's going to happen."

"Okay," said Scarlett. "You guys take that end. We'll stay over here. On the count of three, we'll pull it together."

Molly kicked at some of the things on the floor that were blocking the board. The other girls did the same.

"Ready?" said Scarlett. "One, two, three."

They all pulled. With the full effort of all four of them, they slid the plywood away from the wall. It tipped backwards.

"Heads up!" shouted Molly.

They all jumped out of the way as the board crashed toward the ground, landing loudly on a pile of dirty equipment. A cloud of dust filled the air.

Pooja coughed. "Nasty."

Molly and Scarlett focused their flashlights on the newly exposed wall. It was difficult to make out anything through the haze. Then Molly saw it.

"Holy cow."

"What is it?" asked Daneen.

"It's another message," said Scarlett.

"What does it say?" asked Pooja.

"'Unless, together, they regret,'" she read.

"What the heck does that mean?" asked Pooja.

Molly shined her flashlight on the opposite wall. She read the original message. "'I will never forget.'" Then the new message. "'Unless, together, they regret.'"

Suddenly, a loud screeching noise shook the shed. The four of them turned. Molly and Scarlett shined their flashlights toward the sound.

The door to the shed was closing. And fast.

Scarlett was the first to react. She flew toward the door and caught it just in time. She pushed her entire body weight against the door. "Everybody out, now!" she shouted. "I can't hold it much longer!"

Molly, Pooja, and Daneen bolted for the exit, rushing past Scarlett.

Scarlett then let go of the door and threw her body out onto the grass. *Bam!* The door immediately banged shut.

The four of them lay in a pile just outside the shed. Molly could feel her heart racing. None of them said a word.

Then, finally, Pooja spoke up. "Are we dead?" she asked.

"No, Pooja, we're not dead," said Daneen.

Scarlett started laughing. Molly couldn't help it. She started laughing, too.

Under the stars, on the wet grass, the only thing they could do was laugh.

13

"Do you really think Vivian Cooper wrote that second message?" asked Daneen.

As they sat together outside the shed a few minutes later, they had lots of questions.

"The two messages definitely seem to go together," said Molly. "'I will never forget. Unless, together, they regret.'"

"What do you think it means?" asked Pooja.

"Is it possible we're the first ones to see it?" asked Scarlett.

"The cops could've missed the second message that night when they went into the shed looking for Vivian," said Daneen.

"And that piece of plywood has probably been covering it up for decades," said Scarlett.

"We're the first ones to see it," said Pooja. "Definitely."

"Vivian's referring to the girls from her soccer team, right?" asked Molly. "'Unless *they* regret.' 'They' must mean the other girls."

"They never confessed to locking Vivian in the shed," said Scarlett.

"Just the anonymous note," said Daneen.

"How about later?" asked Molly. "Ten years later? Twenty?"

"The players never confessed," said Scarlett with an edge to her voice. "Ever."

Daneen shrugged. "Except for the rumors and the stories we tell each other on the team, the disappearance of Vivian Cooper is still a mystery in Winchester to this day."

"Those old ladies are going to their graves with what they did to that witch," said Pooja.

"Watch it," said Scarlett.

"What did I say?" asked Pooja.

"She is my aunt, remember?" said Scarlett.

"I'm sorry, but if she wasn't a witch, then

what was she?" said Pooja. "She did put a curse on the shed. She had some kind of freaky powers."

Scarlett shook her head.

"So that's it," said Molly. "In order to break the curse, all we have to do is get the girls from the original soccer team to show remorse for what they did to Vivian and confess to their crime."

Daneen laughed. "Oh, is that all? What could be easier?"

14

Saturday morning, the girls met at the Winchester Public Library. They approached the librarian at the front desk. "Hi," said Molly. "Can you help us get access to issues of the Winchester Gazette from . . ." She turned to Scarlett. "What year did the girls' team get started?"

"1959," said Scarlett.

"From 1959?" Molly asked the librarian.

"Of course," he said. "But those haven't been made digital yet. I'll get you the hard copies." He walked into the back room. When he returned a couple of minutes later, he held twelve large hardcover books in his arms. "One book for every month from 1959," he said, dropping them on the counter.

Each of them grabbed a stack of books and brought them to a long, wooden table on the other side of the library. "Remind me what we're looking for?" asked Daneen.

"Names of the players from that original soccer team," said Molly. "The team was a big deal that year in Winchester, so their names should definitely be in one of these books."

The girls began paging through the books. They started with the warmer months. Molly had May. She passed by pages of wedding announcements and obituaries. Through stories describing the Winchester spring festival, a large spread detailing the graduating class from Winchester High, and a lengthy farm report about the upcoming cranberry crop. There was absolutely nothing about the Winchester girls' soccer team.

She was ready to move to the June book when Pooja bolted upright in her chair. "I found it!"

The girls gathered around her. Sure enough, on the page Pooja had open was a large picture of the team. The players stood in rows, arms around each other, huge smiles on their faces. The names of each of the players were written in the caption below it. A headline above the picture read, *Soccer: Not Just for the Boys.*

"You're darn right," said Pooja, pointing at the headline.

"There they are," said Molly. "Wow. Hard to believe those smiling girls were responsible for something so awful."

"You can't judge a book by its cover," said Scarlett.

"Someone take a picture of it," said Daneen.

Molly got out her phone and snapped a few pictures. She made sure she could read all the names from the caption. "Let's go to a computer."

They gathered around Molly at one of the library computers. "What are the odds any of them are still alive?" asked Daneen. "They'd be like . . ."

"Almost eighty," said Scarlett.

"And there's no way they're all still in Winchester, right?" asked Daneen.

"Enough with the pessimism," said Molly. "We won't know until we start looking."

Molly checked the picture on her phone then typed in the first name from the caption in the computer's search box. Bess Gardner. She also included the word Winchester in her search. Immediately a social media link came up. Molly clicked on it. A picture of an elderly woman flashed onto the screen. Molly clicked on her profile and saw she still lived in Winchester. *Born: December 17, 1942.* "It's gotta be her," said Molly. "Everything matches. She would've been in high school in 1959."

"That was easy," said Scarlett.

Molly typed in the next name. Sophie Beringer. Again, a profile popped up. Same thing. She lived in Winchester. She was born in 1942.

Molly searched the third name on the list. This time she came back with nothing. The next name. Again, nothing that matched a woman from Winchester. "You know," said Daneen. "Most of them probably got married and changed their names."

"Good point." Molly continued through the list. Scarlett jotted notes in her phone as she went. By the end, they had found four of the girls in the photo still alive and still living in Winchester. They found absolutely nothing on the remaining eleven.

Molly sat back in her chair. "It's a start." She looked back at the others. "What's next?"

"I say we start with the first one we found," said Scarlett looking at her phone. "Bess Gardner."

15

Thirty minutes later, Molly stood with Scarlett on the front porch of Bess Gardner's house. Daneen and Pooja had stayed back at the library to track down more information about the rest of the 1959 team.

Molly was nervous. "How are we going to do this?" she asked. "What are we going to ask her?"

"I say we just go for it," said Scarlett. "I don't think there's much we can do to prepare."

Molly took a deep breath. Then she rang the bell.

They heard footsteps inside the house, then seconds later a woman appeared at the door.

Molly recognized her from her social media picture. "Hello?" the woman asked.

Molly looked at Scarlett. Then back at the woman. "Are you Bess Gardner?"

"Yes," said Bess.

"Hi. My name's Molly and this is my friend Scarlett. We were wondering if we could talk with you for a minute."

"What's this about?" asked Bess with a smile.

Molly hesitated for a moment. She could dance around why they were there. She could beat around the bush for a while and be friendly. Instead she decided to be direct. "We know about Vivian Cooper," she said. "We know what the soccer team did to her back in 1959."

The smile on Bess' face disappeared. "I'm afraid I don't know what you're talking about." She began to close the door. Molly reached out to stop it.

"We know about the shed," said Molly. "We know you left her in there."

Bess stopped.

"We're not here to blame you," said Molly. "We just want to talk. And we think you can help us."

Bess stood in silence, her head sinking toward the floor.

Molly didn't know what to do. She didn't want to barge into this old woman's home. If Bess didn't want to talk to them, there wasn't much they could do about it.

Just then Scarlett stepped forward. "Vivian Cooper was my aunt."

Bess wiped her eyes, then looked up. Tears were rolling down her cheeks.

"My name is Scarlett Cooper."

"Oh dear." Bess began to quiver. She turned and stumbled toward a chair in the entryway.

Molly and Scarlett rushed toward her. They helped her into the chair.

Bess sat crying and breathing heavily. Finally she looked up at the girls. "I knew this moment would come one day," she said. She reached out and took Molly and Scarlett's hands.

Several minutes later, the three of them sat together at Bess' kitchen table. She had put out some tea and cookies.

"You don't know how long I've been waiting for this day," said Bess. "I've been living with the burden of what we did to that poor girl my whole life."

"Why didn't you tell anyone?" asked Molly.

"Or go to the police?" asked Scarlett. "You could've confessed."

"I couldn't get myself to do it," said Bess. "All these years and I've done nothing. I didn't think the police would believe me. Especially as I became older. You have to remember, they never found Vivian. Why would they believe me that she somehow just vanished from the shed? They would think I'm just some crazy old woman."

"What do you think happened to Vivian?" asked Molly.

"Something awful," said Bess. "We put her in that shed and locked the door. We were the only ones with the key. There's no way she got out of there alive." Bess shook her head and let out a big sigh. Molly reached for a tissue from a box on the table and handed it to her. "Thank you, dear."

"We think we've found a way for you to atone for what you did," said Molly. "A way for the whole team to finally give Vivian the peace she deserves."

"We found a second message in the shed," said Scarlett.

"So it's true," said Bess. "Players from the soccer team can still see the shed."

"We can," said Molly.

"I've heard rumors through the years."

"Not only can we see the shed," said Scarlett. "Molly got trapped inside. She almost didn't make it out alive."

"Oh dear," said Bess.

"We need to end the curse," said Molly. "We don't want anything bad to happen to anyone else."

Scarlett continued. "The second message in the shed says, 'Unless, together, they regret.'"

"You know what that means, right?" asked Molly.

Bess rubbed her eyes with the tissue. "I think it's pretty clear. My teammates and I must confess to what we did. Once and for all."

Molly nodded. "That's what we think, too."

"If we do that . . ." Bess paused.

"Then Vivian can finally move on and her curse will be broken forever," said Molly. She reached over and gave Bess' hand a squeeze. Bess managed a weak smile. "But it's not possible that all the girls from the soccer team are still alive, is it?"

Bess smiled. "I believe they are. I haven't heard of any of them passing away."

"I think Vivian has kept you all alive so you can finally do what you should've done years ago," said Scarlett with an edge to her voice.

Bess's smile faded.

Scarlett stood up and walked to the other side of the room. She was clearly agitated. "What I'm trying to say is I can't believe you guys did that to my aunt and then pretended like it never happened. For sixty years."

"Scarlett," protested Molly. "You shouldn't . . ."

"It's okay," Bess interrupted. "She has every right to be angry. What we did to that poor, frightened girl was an awful thing. Just awful. I'm not sure we deserve forgiveness." Tears streaked down her cheeks.

"Do you know where any of the players are?" asked Molly.

"Most of them still live in Winchester," said Bess. "The others are close by, I think." She dabbed at her eyes. "But since the day we all graduated from high school, I haven't spoken to even one of them."

"Why?" asked Molly.

"As far as I know," said Bess. "None of us have ever spoken to one another since high school. The burden of what we did to Vivian is too strong. Talking would bring back too many memories. I see some of them around town. At the grocery store or at the café. But we ignore each other. We don't even say 'hello.'" Bess buried her head in her hands. Molly reached out to pat her shoulder.

"I don't know if I can talk to them," Bess continued. "I wish I could. We were like family. But I'm scared. I've buried the events of that day deep inside my soul for a long time. I can still see the terrified look on Vivian's face when we left her in that shed. I don't want to relive that again."

"Vivian lived through much worse," snapped Scarlett. "You shut that door and went on with your life. Vivian never again saw the light of day."

"You're right," said Bess. "Of course you're right."

"We need you to help us," said Molly. "We need you to be strong."

Bess took a deep breath. She looked at Scarlett, then at Molly. She exhaled. "I honestly don't know if I have the strength or courage to help you girls. But I'll try my best. I make that promise to you."

"Thank you Bess," said Molly.

"It's the least I can do for Vivian," said Bess. She sat up as straight as she could. "Tell me what you need me to do."

16

Together they hatched a plan. And for the next several days Molly and Scarlett helped Bess reach out to each and every one of her former teammates. The process was nearly identical with every player. Initially each woman was resistant to help. They were resistant to even talk about what they had done to Vivian. It was Scarlett who finally convinced them by telling them all her personal story of her aunt and how what happened to Vivian has stuck with the Cooper family to this day. One by one, through tears and the recall of painful memories, Scarlett, Molly, and Bess helped every former Whitecaps player come to the same conclusion. They needed to confess to their crime. They needed to come clean to the city of Winchester regardless of what legal punishment lay before them.

After getting all the players on board, Molly and Scarlett scheduled a press conference at city hall where the 1959 team would declare what they had done to Vivian. Molly knew the public confession would not be easy. And she had no idea if their plan would really lift the curse. But they had come this far and there was no turning back now.

The same day as the press conference, Molly and her teammates were back home, facing off against the Smithfield Red Hawks.

From the start of the game, things did not go well. The Red Hawks controlled play as Molly and her teammates did nothing but frantically chase the ball from sideline to sideline. They managed to tackle the ball away from time to time but could not keep control or muster even one serious scoring opportunity.

Ten minutes into the game the Red Hawks scored. And to make matters worse, while trying to stop the ball, the Winchester goalie made an awkward play and landed hard on her shoulder. She had to be removed from the game. *Nice try, Vivian,* Molly told herself. *But we're not going to let your curse stop us. Not today.*

When the new Whitecaps goalie was ready, the team took the kick off. The ball was sent to the right sideline, then to Pooja just across the midline. She attempted to trap the ball but misplayed it out of bounds. "Come on!" she shouted at herself.

The Red Hawks once again had control. Molly crept backwards a bit to provide some defensive support. She marked a player from the Red Hawks. The one who had scored the first goal.

The defenders from the Red Hawks passed the ball back and forth between them as they methodically moved the ball forward toward the center circle. Molly was impressed. Every move they made, every pass, seemed orchestrated.

Daneen attempted to intercept a pass. She was a split second too slow and quickly became out of position. The Red Hawks took advantage. They moved the ball forward, and then the Red Hawk with the ball sent a pass all the way across the field. The ball landed at the feet of a Red Hawk player. Molly sprang forward, hoping to catch the girl off guard, but the Red Hawk quickly dribbled forward along the sidelines, racing past Molly.

The rest of the action happened quickly. The ball was sent into the corner where a Red Hawk trapped it, then kicked it high into the box. Molly tried her best to scramble back, but she was well behind the action.

A group of players near the goal converged on the ball as it sailed toward them. A couple of Red Hawks forwards, several Whitecaps defenders, and the new Whitecaps goalie all jumped high into the air.

Thump!

A collision. It was loud. And it was awful. It was the sound of two heads banging violently together.

It happened a lot in soccer. And it was never pretty. But this one sounded louder than any other Molly could remember. *Vivian!* Molly screamed inside. *Stop it already! Don't you know we're trying to help you?*

As the ball was cleared harmlessly across the end line, two players lay sprawled on the ground. One was the previous goal scorer from the Red Hawks. The other was the backup Whitecaps goalie.

Molly rushed over. The goalie was clearly in severe pain. She was holding her hands across her right eye. There was blood trickling down the side of her face. Coach Rogers raced to her side, along with the referee.

Molly, like the other players around her, took a knee and watched as Coach Rogers attended to her teammate. The JV team had just arrived after completing their game, and all of their players looked on from the sidelines. Scarlett and Molly made eye contact. They both shook their heads. *Stupid curse*, thought Molly. She knew Scarlett was thinking the same thing.

The goalie was finally escorted from the field. Players from the varsity and JV and fans in the crowd applauded. Once she was on the sidelines, the girl's parents immediately helped her toward the parking lot. Molly suspected they were on their way to the emergency room.

The remaining Whitecaps finally got to their feet and gathered in the middle of the field. "Now what are we going to do?" asked Pooja as she, Daneen, and Molly stood together. There weren't any other goalies on the varsity team.

Molly looked to the sidelines. She then looked back at her teammates. She smiled. "I have an idea."

17

It took some arm-twisting to convince Coach Rogers of Molly's idea: put Scarlett in. She was there, just sitting in the stands. Ready and waiting.

"Give her a chance, Coach," Molly said. "She deserves it. She's been working hard in practice, right? And playing really well in JV games."

"I will say, her attitude has gotten a lot better," admitted Coach Rogers, crossing her arms. She took a breath, then nodded her head. "I'll give her a shot. But I better not regret this."

"Yes!" Molly ran into the stands and broke the news to Scarlett.

"What?" said Scarlett. "Are you serious? How in the world . . . ?"

Molly interrupted. "No time for questions. You need to get onto the field before Coach Rogers changes her mind."

Scarlett smiled, then scrambled down the bleachers. She raced quickly into goal.

Molly, Pooja, and Daneen helped her warm up.

"We're glad you're finally part of the varsity!" shouted Daneen, firing a shot at her. Scarlett stopped it, then rolled the ball back toward them.

Pooja kicked it hard toward the goal. "Do you think you can shut down these Red Hawks?"

Scarlett stopped that shot too. "I know I can."

After getting Scarlett warmed up, Molly, Daneen and Pooja returned to their positions. The game resumed.

The Red Hawk in the corner kicked the ball toward the box. One of her teammates timed her leap perfectly and blasted a header on goal. Scarlett pounced. She dove through the air, fully extending her body, and snatched the ball with both hands before crashing to the ground.

"Yes!" said Pooja.

"Here we go!" called Daneen.

Scarlett immediately rolled the ball out toward a Whitecaps player who took the pass and began to dribble up the field. The Red Hawks quickly moved back to defend. "Open!" called Molly. She got the ball in stride and dribbled quickly ahead, keeping her eyes on her teammates on either side of her.

But then a Red Hawk came in from the side and snatched the ball away. The Red Hawk edged into the corner, dancing back and forth with the ball, looking for the right timing to make the perfect pass. She kicked the ball wide, then sent a pass into the box.

Scarlett pounced. Instead of waiting for another Red Hawk to get her foot on the ball and take a shot, she rushed forward in the box and snatched the ball cleanly out of the air. Several Red Hawks around her looked stunned that she had come out and made such a bold, aggressive play.

But Scarlett wasn't satisfied with the save. She immediately dropped the ball and kicked it hard and long toward the middle of the field. She had spotted Pooja, cheating back toward the Red Hawks' goal.

Pooja broke for the ball. Except for the goalie, there wasn't one single Red Hawk between her and the goal. Pooja sprinted forward while all the other players ran to catch up. Molly was so far behind the action that all she could do was watch.

The goalie was putty in Pooja's hands. Pooja stutter-stepped, then bobbed her head and shoulders to the left. The goalie bit. Pooja then effortlessly slid around her to the right, looked at the open goal, and sent a confident shot forward.

The ball sailed easily and beautifully into the back of the net.

The game was tied 1–1.

The Whitecaps players cheered and ran toward Pooja.

Molly raced over to Scarlett. "How in the world did you see her like that?"

"It's a goalie's job," she said. "Stop the other team but keep your head up so you can help your own team attack."

"Brilliant," said Molly.

The scored remained 1–1 well into the second half. The Whitecaps managed a couple more scoring opportunities but couldn't put the ball in the goal. Meanwhile, Scarlett rose to the occasion and stopped three more shots on goal.

It all came down to the last five minutes.

Molly found herself alone in the middle of the field with the ball on her foot. *Midfielders are the most important players on the soccer field,* she thought. *Midfielders help stop the other team's attackers. They make the best passes. And they set up other players for scoring opportunities.* A defender stood several yards in front of her, waiting for Molly to make a move. Molly dribbled slowly forward. She then looked to her right. Daneen was running up the sidelines. Molly looked to her left. Pooja was there, waving her arm for the ball. Finally, Molly looked straight ahead of her. Past the defender. She looked at the goal. It was beautiful. The white lace of the net shined in the setting sun. It looked so big. Molly quickly made up her mind. *But sometimes*, she thought, *midfielders attack!*

Molly made a jab step to her left, then flashed past her defender to the right. Another defender approached. Molly flicked the ball a couple feet into the air, avoiding the leg of the defender, then continued forward. She could see the goalie taking a few steps out of the goal. Molly had a clear shot. Yes, she was still thirty feet from the goal, but if she placed the ball just right, she was confident she could score. Molly pulled her right leg back, then let it fly. The ball flew through the air in a beautiful arc. The goalie jumped high, diving diagonally. The ball sailed past the goalie's outstretched fingers and into the top corner of the goal.

The other girls swarmed her. "That was amazing!" screamed Daneen.

Pooja lifted her off the ground. "Where have you been hiding that leg all this time?" she laughed.

Molly broke from the group and looked back at Scarlett. Scarlett pumped her fist high into the air. The smile on her face was the widest Molly had ever seen.

In that instant, the referee blew her whistle. The game was over.

Molly and Scarlett raced together toward the group that had swarmed around Pooja. The Whitecaps were all cheering and congratulating each other.

Pooja gave Scarlett a shove. "Nice pass."

"Nice finish," replied Scarlett. "I think we just showed Aunt Vivian her curse can't stop us anymore."

"That's right!" said Molly.

"If Coach tries keeping you off the varsity team any longer," said Pooja. "There's going to be a revolt."

"An all-out rebellion," laughed Daneen.

Molly looked at the sky. The sun was nearing the horizon. "I'd love to stay here and celebrate this win all night, but . . ."

"We have a press conference to get to," said Daneen.

"And curse to break," said Pooja.

"That's right," said Molly. "You all ready for this?"

The four of them locked arms.

"Let's do this thing," said Scarlett.

18

The four girls walked into the atrium inside Winchester City Hall. Molly couldn't believe the scene in front of them. The place was packed. Nearly every chair was taken, and people were lined up shoulder to shoulder along the back wall. Journalists with professional cameras stood near the front. On the stage was a long table with over a dozen empty chairs.

As the girls made their way toward the back of the room, they passed a table with coffee and cookies. Pooja grabbed a cookie and stuffed it into her mouth. "How can you eat at a time like this?" asked Daneen over the sound of the crowd.

"I'm hungry," said Pooja between mouthfuls.

As the girls squeezed together into an empty corner, Bess stepped onto the stage. She was followed by a small group of elderly women. Two of them were in wheelchairs. One walked with a cane. They were all the former members of the first Whitecaps team. Joining them on stage were four uniformed police officers. The crowd suddenly went silent.

"They're actually going to do it," whispered Molly.

"They better," said Scarlett. "No backing out now."

"I don't know if I can watch," said Molly.

Bess and the other women settled at the table. The audience was frozen. All eyes were locked on the former Winchester players.

Bess tapped on the microphone in front of her. A series of thuds echoed from the speakers near the stage. Bess scooted forward in her chair. She cleared her throat. "Ladies and gentlemen, thank you for coming."

Molly looked at her friends.

"We called together this press conference for a very important reason," Bess continued. "Believe it or not, my fellow teammates and I have not spoken to each other in over sixty years. We've been silent. And we've been cowards. We've kept a secret from this community for a very long time regarding an awful thing we did to one of our classmates back in high school.

"Two things happened in this town back in 1959," said Bess. "One was magical. The emergence of the first all-girls soccer team in the state. The other was horrible. The disappearance of Vivian Cooper."

Members of the audience began shifting in their chairs. The reality of what Bess was about to say was clearly beginning to make some people uncomfortable.

"And all of us on this stage were responsible for both," said Bess. "We caused the disappearance of Vivian Cooper." A murmur came out from the audience. "We locked her in that shed and left her there. We are the reason she vanished from Winchester forever."

People began to turn to one another. A hum of whispers and gasps filled the room.

Bess reached out and grabbed the hands of the two women next to her. "There's something all of us need to do here today," she said loudly, attempting to regain the audience's attention. "Ladies?" She looked down to the end of the table.

The woman at the end sat up straight. "I locked Vivian Cooper in that shed," she said in her loudest voice.

The woman to her left was next. "I locked Vivian Cooper in that shed."

One by one, down the line, each woman said the same thing. "I locked Vivian Cooper in that shed."

The room was silent as each and every member of the original Winchester girls' soccer team admitted to what they did to Vivian on that fall day back in 1959.

"We did an awful, awful thing to that girl," said Bess. "No one knows exactly what happened to Vivian. But we take responsibility for locking her in the shed and forcing her to suffer alone. For days." She looked at her teammates. "We acknowledge our crime and we're here tonight to turn ourselves over to the police. We accept whatever punishment we deserve.

"But most of all," Bess continued, looking at the audience. "We want to apologize to the family of Vivian Cooper and the community of Winchester for the terrible act we committed on that day. We hope you can all find it in your hearts to one day forgive us."

Bess looked down the line. "Ladies?" She stood up. Her teammates slowly followed her off the stage and into a back room. The police officers joined them.

"Let's go," said Molly. She grabbed Scarlett's hand and led the girls onto the stage and toward the back room. An officer was blocking the entrance.

"Let us through," said Molly. "We're Bess' friends."

"No one gets back there," said the officer.

"Please," said Scarlett. "We need to talk to her."

Just then, Molly spotted Bess across the room. She was standing next to a tall officer dressed in a dark blue suit. Bess made eye contact with Molly, then said something to the man. He turned and nodded at the officer in front of the girls.

"I guess you must be important." The officer stepped aside.

The girls rushed over to Bess. Molly embraced her in a hug. "We're so proud of you."

"You were great up there," said Pooja. "Seriously. Thank you."

Bess started crying.

"What is it?" asked Molly.

"I'm no hero," said Bess. "We're not heroes. We should've done this a long time ago."

"What matters is you did it now," said Scarlett.

"That's right," said Daneen.

Molly stepped forward and wrapped her arms around Bess. After a long hug, Molly said, "We'd like to stay and meet the ladies from the team. But there's one last thing we need to do."

"I know," said Bess. "You get over to that field and make sure that shed has disappeared. Once and for all."

"Are you ready?" Molly asked her friends.

"Ready," the all said together.

The four of them turned and headed for the door.

19

Ten minutes later, the girls made it to the edge of the field. Molly couldn't believe her eyes.

"The shed's still there," said Daneen. "It's still there."

As they walked across the field, the old shed was standing where it had always been. It was tucked in the bushes, leaning to one side. It appeared as though nothing about it had changed.

"The confession didn't work," said Pooja.

"All of that was for nothing," said Daneen. "We didn't break the curse."

The joy Molly had felt just moments ago quickly drained from her body. She couldn't believe it. The messages in the shed had seemed so clear. The confession should have ended the curse.

The four of them stood together under the moonlight. In front of the shed. In silence.

Molly wondered what they could do next. *Were there more clues? Had they missed another message in the shed?* She felt defeated.

Then she remembered something. Molly remembered how the original Whitecaps team had treated Vivian before they locked her in the shed. She remembered how they'd considered her an outcast. They hadn't accepted her because she was different. They'd been mean and cold and nasty to her. No one had reached out. No one had even tried to be Vivian's friend.

Molly looked over at Scarlett. *Not much has changed*, she thought.

"Pooja," said Molly. "Daneen."

"Yeah?" they said.

"You think Scarlett's pretty cool right?" said Molly. "She's your friend now, isn't she?"

"Of course," said Daneen.

"Totally," said Pooja.

"And you like all of us, don't you?" Molly asked Scarlett.

"I suppose," said Scarlett. "You guys aren't so bad."

"I think Vivian needs to know that," said Molly. "She needs to see it. She needs to see that her niece is okay. We need to show Vivian that the same thing that happened to her sixty years ago is never going to happen to another Cooper girl. Ever."

"What do you want me to do?" asked Scarlett. "Hug you or something?"

"Sure," said Molly. "It can't hurt."

"I don't need people being nice to me just to break the curse," said Scarlett. "How do I know you guys aren't going to start ignoring me again once this is all over?"

"We're friends now," said Molly. "And that's not going to change."

"That's right," said Daneen.

"We want to hang out with you," said Pooja. "The question is, do you want to hang out with us?"

Scarlett shuffled her feet.

"You're just going to have to trust us," said Molly. "We like you for who you are. Yeah, maybe you're not like all the other girls. Maybe you're a little . . ."

"Quirky?" said Pooja.

"But that's why we like you," added Daneen.

"You guys are the quirky ones, if you ask me," said Scarlett.

Molly laughed. "See. Right there. You're funny. We love that about you."

"We've got your back," said Pooja.

"Friends?" asked Daneen, with her arms open.

"Friends?" asked Pooja.

Scarlett stood in silence. "You've got to be kidding me."

The three of them waited.

Then Scarlett looked at each of them. One after the other.

Finally, she shook her head and smiled. "Oh, all right. Friends." She walked toward Molly, Pooja, and Daneen.

The three of them embraced her in a tight hug.

When it was over, they stood together, hand-in-hand in front of the shed.

No one said a word. They waited.

Molly felt herself breathing softly. Her heart rate was slow. She was calm.

Molly felt Scarlett squeeze her hand. "We're so sorry Vivian," she said. "For everything that happened to you."

"It's time Aunt Vivian," said Scarlett. "It's time to forgive this town. To forgive the players."

More silence.

Then Molly felt a breeze pass over her. A warm, soft breeze. It brushed over her face, though her hair then down her body.

"Did you feel that?" asked Molly.

"I did," said Scarlett.

Then, before their eyes, the shed began to slowly vanish. First the roof. Then the walls.

Finally, the shed was gone. In its place was a tangled bramble of bushes, as if nothing else had been there for decades.

"Thank you, Aunt Vivian," said Scarlett. "Thank you. May you finally rest in peace."

Molly looked at Scarlett. She wrapped her arm around Scarlett's shoulder. "It's done."

Scarlett did not pull away. She wrapped her arm around Molly and gave her one, solitary nod of the head. "It's finally done."

ABOUT THE AUTHOR

Along with being a writer, Chris Kreie is an elementary English teacher. He also spent over a decade as a school librarian, a profession he loved. He lives in Minneapolis, Minnesota with his wife, two children, a dog and a cat. His interests away from writing include hiking in the woods, biking the fabulous Twin Cities trail system and kayaking down the beautiful Minnehaha Creek that flows through his neighborhood.